David Sims was living his life the best way he knew how too . He had a great job and also he was loving this new raise he had gotten . He also was happy about looking into the future with his soon to be bride Giovanni Reid who was an recent lawyer who was trying to get her practice off the ground.

So far with the helped of David, things were going good for them both their careers were going in the direction that they wanted them too . Thank god is what Giovanni response was .

. He was happy he had a strong , beautiful and talented woman on his arm . He knew from the moment he saw her that she was the one for him .

He decided to celebrate his new deal with Giovanni ,his partners , family and friends . This was what he had been wanting and this was something that he had seen in the future but didn't expect it right now .

Not only was David a force to be reckoned with but he was on his way to the top . He decided to go to Juan's a popular soul food place to celebrate his promotion and business deal that went through this morning .

Giovanni was so proud of the man who was soon to be her husband everything was working out for them and for their good . Life was good and NOTHING could ruined that for her or her mood . She was feeling the excitement along with David and you could tell life had new meaning by this night.

David and Giovanni decided tonight they wouldn't drink but they would drink when they got to their beautiful home they shared . David nodded when his beautiful fiancé had said what she did . She knew things would be alright for them and couldn't wait for their future together .

She kept saying Mrs Giovanni Reid Sims hmmmm love the ring to that and all . Things were going well and this is what they really did want .

As they turn onto the corner on 45th and 9th Giovanni had a weird feeling in her stomach . Like something was about to happen . As they turn right David forgot there was an stop sign there .

Then all the sudden they see blue lights behind then so David looks at Giovanni and says everything will be alright my love and hold her hands . He turns off in a parking lot and make sure their was lighting .

He then stops and gets his registration out and his driver license out and he does crack his window and all before the policemen comes and ask for them . David tells Giovanni to stay calm and this would be over fast . Those words pained

Giovanni so much and it really makes her

think about them .

   The officer who walk to the door of his

car opens the door without identifying

himself and with an attitude began to

questioned David .

   David and the officer have some heated

words with his hand clear view , so that

they can see them and not get killed . All of

the sudden this traffic stop takes a turn for

the worse when the cop went from being calm to being in rage and then things went left where Mr Sims lays on the ground shot fourteen times and his girlfriend and fiancé Miss Reid in the car screaming and crying as she is seeing this unfold in front of her .

This is a dream she said while watching this scene this can't be real at all . Heart beating out her chest and her breath was heavy and couldn't moved at all . She felt helpless in the situation .

What did David do and why was David a victim of another hashtag . He deserves better than that . Soon more police officers were on the scene and then the captain came to the side of the car and told Giovanni how sorry he was that this happened .

Immediately they handcuffed the officer who shot him and took him off to jail . With mixed emotions she was numb and didn't understand what was going on at all .

All she knew was the man who she loves was dead and she had no clue what to do next . Say his name Danny Sims .

Another hashtag. Not another BLACK MAN.

Today was the day they were putting David Rasheed Sims to rest . This shouldn't be happening . Here is a person who she loved and David saw the good in everyone . Even in the time of his fatal death he kept telling her he was alright . But the ended of this horrible crime was that David was dead . No more life in him .

No more kisses , no more trips and no more them and no more future . These cops took someone who they love so much and gave so much and his fate was that he was killed in the streets .

They thought a simple apology was going to helped out the matter it made it worse . The family felt like they had been slapped in the face and had no control in what was going on at all .

Giovanni got to pick out the suit he was going to wear in his casket . It was cream trim in gold . So she pick the suit he had plan on wearing to their wedding. She cried as she went to the casket and saw him laying there looking handsome . She was waiting for him to get up and hug her and say this was a joke .

But what hurt Giovanni was seeing his mother crying uncontrollably because she had once again loss another child to violence and she couldn't help him in his time of need . This is something that was racking her brain .

She too was losing the love of her life they met at a local coffee house and couldn't even began to see life without her knight and shining armor . This man was everything that she always want and needed .

Feeling all this hurt was tearing her up and seeing his mother crying over another death of a son hurt her too .

She said finally when will this killing stop . She knew that this had to be fixed . This was the moment she had to be the unapologetic black woman she was born to be .

Three months after the untimely death of her love David Sims the men who were charged with manslaughter and first degree murder the trial was starting . Giovanni knew this was the moment she wasn't looking forward too .

The defense had called her up to the stand to testify in the night in questioning of the death of her fiancé . Hands were sweaty and she was weak . This death has taken a toll on her and her body and she wasn't ready for what was next .

She knew that David would want her to do this. Around her neck she had a necklace of her and David the picture was the night that he had gotten killed . She walk slowly to the stand and looking at David's killers with sadness and looking like she was about to have the whole world looking at her .

But in fact the media had been following her everywhere . She didn't have any privacy anymore and this is what really made her anxiety bad . She just want her life back or half of what it was before this case was all over the news and all . She deserve that much and so did his family too.

Giovanni step on the stand was trembling with fear but she had a job to do and that was tell the truth of what happen that night . She had ask for them to give her some water because her throat was dry . She knew what had to be said for her testimony to be recorded and be actual too . She slowly began that terrified night .

" David and I were engaged she said . That night was supposed to be special because he had gotten that deal and promotion at work that he had work so hard for . " Tears ran down her face and she knew that this was something she

didn't want to talk about .

She was about to tell the horrible

events of that night . She said that they

were eating and celebrating at their

favorite spot she began to cry and the

lawyer came with an tissue and the judge

said that he knew this was hard for her .

She got the strength to go on and tell

what really happened that night the police

officer took her future and mate away .

She had mentioned that David hadn't

drank anything that night in fact they were

waiting until they got home to really celebrate . David wasn't the type to drank anything especially when he was the DD which means he was the designated driver

.

They had turn the corner and David had not notice that their was a stop sign that he had missed . So he proceed to drive until he was seeing blue lights glaring from the back of his window. He then turn to his fiancé and kept reassuring her that everything was going to be alright .

She recalls that the officer had came to the car with a polite manner he wasn't rude or mean at all . He saw that David had all of his items that needed on the dashboard clear view for the officers .

He even had his window completely down and had instructed his fiancé to put her information on the dash and she did without having an attitude or anything at all

.

She said that the police officer said Mr Sims were your aware that you past a stop sign . David replied wasn't no sir I wasn't aware at all . The officer thought he had smell alcohol on his breathe and had him get out the car.

David kept telling me baby it will be alright keep your hands up and don't moved at all . Don't give them a reason to used their guns on you or us . I don't want to be another hashtag in the Black Lives Matters movement baby .

When he said this you could tell that this hurt him to say this . But he was being honest with his opinion of this and what we were dealing with . When he was walking

the line for the breathing test one of the officers hollered at gun and they had their weapons pointing to the head of David .
But David being who he was he said I don't have no gun man.

They proceed to headed to him and he wasn't having it . The officer again said gun and began shooting at my David . She said at this moment she lost it crying and screaming and saying stop shooting my fiancé .

After about ten rounds David fell to the ground bloody and screaming for me .

At that moment I ran to him and the officers didn't stop me they were trying to figure out what happened . One of them call on his radio that they need an ambulance immediately . Then the other who didn't shoot him began CPR on him and telling him to hold on that help was on the way .

I was shocked and mad and angry the one thing he had mentioned to me he was about to be another hashtag . Something he didn't want at all . Then five minutes back and here the ambulance was here and she was running toward David . David now at this point was still alive and they were working on him .

They ask me what happened I said was suppose to be a normal traffic stop because David ran a stop sign and now he is laying here because the officer want to shoot him because they thought he had a gun . So the EMT looked and saw no weapon on David and just kept working on David .

He was crying and saying I don't want to died out here like my brother did . God saved me please . They got him on the stretcher and carried to the local hospital to work on him some more .

David Sims died at 9:45 pm at the hospital they said that he was losing too much blood and that he had crashed twice and they had got him back the first two times but the last time no they couldn't save him . On the stand Giovanni was crying uncontrollably now .

She said I had to witness my love be murdered in front of me and there was absolutely nothing I could do to saved him and it hurts . He will never get that

business deal back , never raised our

future kids and we won't ever be husband

and wife because of this .

This is the part that hurt the most and it

hurt because David was in a casket and

the guilty men were here with their families

and laughing and enjoying each other and

he was another damn hashtag .

David needed justice and he needed a

voice that was going to fight for him when

he needed them the most . Things had

been done wrong and things didn't look

like they were getting better . Giovanni was heartbroken . The words didn't come out right and she didn't expect for the trial to be three long months . But it was and she was seeing how the world was honoring his memory .

They show the body cam and the guilty officer turn away from the video of where he was there arresting David who wasn't doing anything wrong . A cell phone was apparently suppose to be the weapon he pull on the officer for him to defend himself and shot him but come on fourteen times .

Where is the justice in that . Now the groups that came out do this want to know that too . The family was hurting every single day wearing David favorite colors blue and white .

He was a big Tar Heel fan . He bleed them not just loved them . He was a guy who would be the talk at every single barbecue. His family love him and he loved them . But Giovanni couldn't shake this feeling and how she was feeling about what was going on.

HE was DEAD . He was actually GONE ! No more among the living all because someone who was trigger happy officer said he saw a gun and it wasn't even a gun but his cell phone .

He was taking it out to and what injustice was being done to him but he was the main focus of his untimely death .

The attorney then turns to Giovanni I know it has been hard about the passing of someone you love so much . But answered this question " Do you think that he would be alive now if he hadn't reach in his pocket to get his phone "? Giovanni was speechless off the question . But her response was one that the attorneys were shocked too .

Giovanni replies was " Sir if you seen your wife being murdered in front of you and you were told my the officer partner not to get out the car before they shoot you too how would that make you feel "? The attorney said it would hurt me to my core to see someone shooting that many times into my wife .

As the jury went and heard this tears went down each face and even the judge was emotional too . Giovanni said I have a nightmares of that tragic night and can't do anything about it at all . She said that it replays like a bad scene from a movie and things were just NOT ever going to be the same again for her and she knew this .

Not because what the reality was but because she was not happy at all by all this that was going on .

These officers had the opportunity to go and be with their families and lived their lives like they should and how David want too . Giovanni was a strong and unapologetic woman not because she was on the stand but because this didn't break her . She was seeing all the love that they were showing her and David's family during this time .

The protest were peaceful in some states and others people were mad by the video that the media had shown them . But the family and Giovanni kept telling them that they need to stop looting and all that it wasn't solving anything at all .

People were wearing shirts with David face on them and saying justice for David Sims let his death not go in vein . Poems were written on his behalf and all . Things were going good except for the fact David was gone .

David was being remembered not as another damn hashtag but the movement to speak his name proudly and let others know here was this man no record and no bad blood with no one and lay on that snowy ground blood pouring out him with his eyes closed .

Giovanni running to him and holding him in her arms and screaming why did you have to killed him ? The officer who shot him had no emotion on his face and just stood there . The other officer call it in . But it was too late his partner Officer Amos Smith has murdered David Sims because he thought he had seen a GUN . Where David didn't own on nor did he want too .

He said owning a gun would get him killed one day . It's seem like he was right about the whole thing now . The world was upset about what was going on and couldn't do anything about it at all .

But this was the American that Giovanni was forced to live in . One she wasn't happy about at all . She was hurt by the same ones who was suppose to served and protect her . But in the end she killed her boyfriend David .

A man full of life and all she knew that this case was being watch by a lot of people and things were finally coming together .

Then for the last few weeks Giovanni seem to be getting bigger and her clothes were getting tight . She is wasn't thinking much about it but then she was . As she looked at herself in the mirror the reality had set in for her AM I PREGNANT? I can't be but then again I think I am .

Tears began to fall from her face and she couldn't stop and then all the sudden her nausea came out of no where and she hadn't seen her period since the morning before all of this happened . She had made a promise to David to get check out and see what was really going on with her

.

But to her surprises she knew what the issue was . She knew this would make David's family happy and his mom a piece of her son would lived on .

Giovanni went to Walgreens and went to purchase a test . It was now or never . She went into the bathroom and took the test and waited for the time that was on the box and she was in fact PREGNANT. She took the other two to be sure and it was true that Giovanni was going to be a MOM.

Tears ran down her face . She had about a hour to get to the courthouse and all but she was feeling awful this morning . But out of no where she heard David sweet voice saying wife go and tend to our baby . I will get the JUSTICE I need and deserved .

She told that sweet spirit. She reached for her phone and called her doctor and see if they could see her this morning and the replied she got back was will 9:55 work . Giovanni said are you soon she went and got into the shower and then put some clothes on and was out the door .

 Giovanni sitting there in the doctor office she was shaking from head to toe . But knew it was just nerves . She was surrounded by other woman who were there . One lady had one child and pregnant with another looking uncomfortable . The other one said she was having infertility problems and was getting shots so she could become a mom . Every woman in this room was strong and their journeys were completely

different to her .

Giovanni Reid her name was called and

it was time to go back there and get the

confirmation that she needed . They drew

blood and had her do a pregnancy test.

Both test came back positive . Giovanni

was in fact pregnant . David was the father

and she cried . The doctor ask did she

want to know how many weeks she was .

Giovanni nodded and the doctor told her

she was 14 weeks along . She could know

the sex of the baby now or she could wait .

She want to know now .

The doctor went and did the ultrasound for her and she was having a girl . The doctor told her to take it easy and did she have anyone going to be with her during this tough time .

She nodded her parents and David's parents and family too . It was a blessing . At that moment she gave her baby the name Isabella Marie Sims . She gave her the name of her daddy to always carried his last name forever .

She took the ultrasound and all with her she was headed to David's parents house to give them the good news . The doctor told her to get by the pharmacy to get her medicine . She nodded and was told congratulations again .

She smiled and then she thought back to the comment that David made telling her she looked like she was gaining weight and now she knew what he was trying her she was carrying his baby . Best feeling in the world and now she wish her sweetheart happy was here with her to celebrate this great news .

Giovanni arrived at David's parents house and they open the door with a smile on their face . Giovanni said hey mama and dad and they hug her . She told them she had something important to tell them .

I just left the doctor and found out that I'm 14 weeks pregnant and I'm having a girl . His mom got up and smile and screaming with joy . I'm going to be a grandmother again oh Giovanni. His dad was happy but they both look at me and said David would be happy to be a father .

He would have been a great one . She also told them that she would be named Isabella Marie Sims they were happy about the name and all . This was joyous celebration for their family and couldn't wait til the little angel made her appearance. Giovanni was shocked that they took this news well and she still had to tell her own parents . But was happy with the baby growing inside of her and she couldn't help to shed a few happy tears and all . Giovanni was on her way to her parents house to tell them the great news .

There had been a continuous in the case dealing with David . More information was coming in and they were waiting on it . As Giovanni was riding in the car she heard the radio station mentioned her love . How this man had no record and the officer shot him like he was an stray dog .

But the fact of the matter was that David was GONE . Giovanni heard on the radio a song made her think about her love which was Steady Love by Indie Arie . She sang with the song and it made her happy she was seat dancing and the tears went away

.

She said the day before this tragic day they had went dancing and this was the song that was being played . They were just two lovebirds and Giovanni was happy.

She had some memories that she could share with their babygirl . She smile as she reach her parents house . They were out in the garden missing with the vegetables and fruits they had planted . She loves this about that about them . How they would just teach her things she could possibly passed to her own baby . Here was the moment of truth and she was excited with them .

All these things she said hurt everybody . But what she said out her mouth shocked everyone . She said David would want us to forgive you for what you did to him . But I just want you to accept your fate and admitted that you killed my son David Sims who was unarmed with NO gun .

She drove down the streets to Juan's

and got her and growing baby some food .

She was trying to get back to her norm but

then she asked what was that .

She got her food and was headed back

to her car when David mama call her and

informed her that the trial goes back

tomorrow . She was silent but his mama

knew what that meant and she said

everything is going to be alright with you

and my granddaughter I promise you that .

In a way Giovanni needed that

reassurance and it came at the right moment like it needed too . God was helping her get through it and all .

The next day in the courtroom they were two days away from closing remarks and all . The attorneys looked they were in the battlefield and all trying to make sure the jury was on their side like Nationwide .

You could tell each jury was listening to both sides and seeing looked as puzzled as the family as to why they shot him that many times while he was down and unarmed which was later determined too .

That puzzled them very much and all . But I guess that's what the attorneys and judges got paid the amount of money they had .

The call one the witnesses who was outside when this all went down . Same story Giovanni said that's what they saw and they said the way that man kept shooting he was enjoying every bullet that was entering into the unarmed black man . He was in the ground pleading and begging and he just took his life in front of his girlfriend . It hurt because no one would want their loved one in that boat at all .

The attorney ask why didn't she tell him to stop and he replied was this " because at first I thought I was in a live action movie with all the violence and all . Being in that neighborhood I have never seen anyone be done like that .

I do regret not helping but the look in that police man face made me think twice if I did who would have said he would've have killed me in front of my children and all . But the attorney was on the officer side just was shocked . No further

questions .

    Giovanni went to the woman who watch

the stuff and all and told her thank you .

She apologizes for not helping her when

she needed her . Giovanni replies was no

apology because they could've killed you

too . She said I will be praying for you and

your family and the baby . Also

congratulations on the new baby I knew he

would have been happy . Confirmation is

what Giovanni replies . The lady look

confused but then smile and left the courtroom .

The attorney for the family said that the partner of the officer was coming up tomorrow and testify. Giovanni felt weird because that was the man who held her while his partner killed David . Sad night for them both but all he got was fired .

The officer after it happened want to tell her sorry about her loss and all Giovanni want from him was why you didn't helped my David out when you took an oath to protect and served and you stood there and did nothing . The officer kept saying I should've done something and maybe he would've have been alive . Replaying what was said to her helped her better understand what was going on . This officer is afraid to face the truth and his part in this crime .

The officer on the stand was quite and kept messing with his hands . He was nervous and also knew he was guilty . But he said his part in this murder of David Sims . This had gotten national attention and all . The officer said " That he felt partly to bone of not stopping this death from happening and then he apologized to the family and said I'm deeply sorry even though I didn't pull the trigger I stood back and did nothing .

David's family nodded to the officers meaning that they understood his response on his part in the murdered of David Sims . At this time Giovanni had tears rolling down her cheek and she was just sad by all of this . Spend all that time with David and to see him get killed by the police officer hurt her heart . Their child would NEVER know her daddy at all . This was something that she didn't quite understand why this happened and how they got to this point .

The officer said he felt bad but by him not doing nothing that he was just as guilty as the officer who shot him to death . The family looked at him and they knew he was sorry because this man said " Mr David will never see his unborn child and won't get married we did this to him " . The family all had tears .

Even though the BLM movement was going strong and all . The family want justice for David . To let the world know they were loved and appreciate and didn't have to worried any longer about getting shot to death and being another hashtag.

They were literally tired of being hashtags and tired of burying their loved ones . Since the death of David so many people have offer yo help out the family and give little Isabella scholarships so that she can go to college and make something of herself .

Giovanni look at David mom and try to see where she was getting this peace from . It had to be nobody but God . No matter what she was going through she knew David would live on through her and little Isabella too . Giovanni said to her self that her mate left her the best gift ever a baby they both helped created together . He would always be with them and protect them at all cost .

Her mama welcomed her with open arms and mentioned that she looked like she is gaining some weight . Her mama was about image and all and she was one who would point out the truth no matter what . She had no filter at all .

Her daddy hushing his wife came and gave his daughter a hug .

You have to consider the stress she has been under during all of this and it has taken a toll on her body . Giovanni laughed at that and said that was funny even from the sky she still smiled over David and his wonderfulness nobody but God .

In Giovanni mind she want her daughter to be a lawyer so that way she can helped out someone who needs the help the possibly was endless but it was something that she was looking forward to .

Back to the courtroom they called David's mom . To see this woman on the stand was very powerful . She spoke with so much knowledge and pain at the same time . But her words were real and true .

" My son was a smart , funny , supportive , and a proud black man . I'm saddened by his passing . On the day that he died he had spend the morning with me talking about how this new business deal is what he needed and what his family needed too . He talk to me about his future and where he want to be and all . He y'all about the wedding that was happening and how he had been waiting for years to see his beautiful bride walk down the aisle to him".

" He was filled with a lot of things and wanting to helped out everyone he could . Seeing my son be the man he always want to be was amazing . He always put the needs of others first and then would focus on himself . My baby laying in his casket

lifeless and dead . Was something I

wouldn't have wish on anybody losing a

child that they loved . The sad thing about

the whole thing was that he dialed my

number . I heard it all my baby begging

this officer to not shoot him .

Then she looked at the officer he

begged you for five minutes and told you

the truth and then you took your gun and

killed my child . Why so many rounds in his

chest . He will never get to be an father

like you had the opportunity too . He won't

get to be the husband you took from him .

He won't even get to grow old and be with

his bride like he plan on forever because

once again you took that from him . He

was only 36 years old . Sir you took our

cheerleader away from us .

Hearing my son crying and begging was

heart breaking . He told you the truth my

son never carried a gun but he knew if he

was in trouble to call his mother . That's

what he was doing when you shoot him .

While he was down you continue on . He

hollered for me . I was on my way then

when I heard you shooting my son on the

phone . I couldn't get on my shoes fast

enough to saved his life . What chilling part

of all of this is when I heard his future

screaming they killed my David .

The jury and all stop and look at David

mom she had heard the men killed her son

. She said my baby laying there in that cold

snow and not moving and not saying

mama I'm alright nothing . You took him

away in a body bag .

After his mama testimony they attorneys

were ready for their closing remarks on the

case . The ones they were defending the officers said this " For the past few weeks we have heard testimonies from a lot of people . But we are here to see if Officer Dean Reston and Officer Matt Ordeal are guilty of first degree murder .

" These officers play a role in the killing and shooting death of Mr David Sims . Who lay lifeless on the cold snow ground . This event happens a few months ago . Are they sad about what happened yes they are .

Do they sympathized with the family of David Sims and friends . The answer is yes but was their shooting him justified? He paused and said yes it was they felt threatened and felt like this man had a gun in his coat pocket ready to ended their lives instead of David going home to his own family and future wife too .

The jury I asked that all charges against them be dismissed and that these officers get back to their lives and be the citizens they needed to be . They have suffered during this ordeal too .

They have received death threats and their families too . They emotionally couldn't handle this case for these many weeks that it has been going on and all .

The jury shook their heads in shocked because for once they was enough evidence to convince them both of all charges . Now it was time for the other attorney to get his time to explain why they deserve this sentence.

The other attorney got up and stood there for a moment . Then began his closing arguments " To the jury you have heard all of the evidence that was presented by myself and the other other attorney . David Sims didn't deserve to died .

He didn't even have a gun and he wasn't even armed . A cell phone was in the pocket of David and instead of the officer asking him to removed his hand from his pocket he open fired on David multiple times .

Then he didn't show any remorse to him and his family or his fiancé or unborn child . David didn't deserve any of this . He was black man who stop like he was suppose too and the other stuff wasn't even suppose to have happened to him . The officers involved didn't do any more to helped him and even threaten his partner while sitting in the car . The pain that the family had to endure was the toughest thing they had to deal with . David will never get a shot to be the husband and father that he really want to be . All because these fatal shots ended his life and now he can't come back from this horrible crime .

I'm asking on the behalf of the David Sims family that you find these officers guilty of the crime they have committed . They knew what they were doing and they also knew that this man wasn't a threat at all .

David was a friendly and honest man who was out to celebrate a deal he had been working on so hard . He didn't ask for this and he didn't want this . He had to reassure her that everything was going to be fine . His last words to his beautiful fiancé . She will always remember this night for the rest of her night .

Find them guilty the family needs justice and David Sims needs it too . He was just so full of life and from what was said today this man served no crime record and no background that was skeptical. The jury was looking at the attorney but what he was saying was true . He knew justice had to be served and it line right there with the people in that courtroom too .

It took the jury about a whole day to come up with the decision. Back and forth and hang jury twice but that last time ended up being the same decision as everyone else . Giovanni and the family got the call to come to the courthouse they had reach the verdict .

At that moment Giovanni stomach got butterflies in them . But she knew it was the baby . She knew what she was feeling so was her unborn little girl too . They had been waiting for this verdict for so long . They knew things would be oh okay eventually and they could try their best to get on with their lives .

It was 9:45 am that morning and it was storming outside too . But looking out the court window they saw the large crowd with umbrellas and all shouting JUSTICE FOR DAVID SIMS ! It was a beautiful thing to see but also they knew this verdict would be the only things to not cause a big riot outside the courthouse for these people for going off and rioting .

Then the head juror stood up and the judge asked have you reach a verdict . In the case at hand we the jury find both defendants GULITY . They would be found

GULITY of all charges first degree murder , manslaughter, using deadly force . They would be sentenced to 30 to 50 years in jail .

   The family look at the lawyer and he assure him that they will be very old man when they do get out of jail . The family clap and thank the jurors for their time . The family in a way got justice for the death of David Sims . Justice was served that day . But all Giovanni could do is cried her eyes out . In her mind it felt like David knew this would happened .

Now she said to herself my handsome hubby to be you will be able to finally Rest In Peace . I will be missing daily because I can no longer hold you and be there for you through all of your business ideas .

So now that we have came to the put about where they were David got justice and the sentence meant they would never get out of jail . He wasn't another hashtag at all . But he was an hero . He had beat the system and finally not like the others who got killed his murders were accused and tired .

So then the family went outside where they were greeted by every news channel and camera taking a picture . The news people were ready for whatever the family had to say . So then out of the people standing Mary Sims spoken and told them this

" Today justice was served for my baby . David got his justice and the ones who were responsible for his death are going to jail for a long time . I'm no longer afraid for the future . David's memories will lived on through his family and friends and his little unborn child Isabella Sims .

The reporter ask Giovanni did she have anything to say . She look at David mom and she nodded and said go on baby it is alright . Then she spoken " My David meant the world to me and now I'm carrying our baby . She will know a lot about her dad and what he did in order for her to be here .

That my heart still hurts and now I can't get the image of him dying on that cold snow street . Myself feeling numb and couldn't helped him when he was literally screaming .

But I know that my love will missed the birth of our daughter but she will know how much I love her daddy and how much he wishes he could have been here during this time . Then they ask the question she knew she wasn't ready for Miss Giovanni what now ?

As a gust of water came from below her and she look down as that question was being asked her water breaks . On nation tv and she was like not now babygirl . But

David mama was like baby it is now . She said ended of questions because we have a grand baby to deliver .

Giovanni was about four weeks early . She kept on apologizing but David's mama was like baby hold on now . Let us take care of you and the baby . They had a police escort to the hospital going fast and all .

Giovanni was breathing hard and all . She knew things would get worser . Then she saw Mary and she said hold on baby . Now breath and relax and I know your hurting not the way we want to bring Isabella in the world but this is God will .

Giovanni said it's probably David's will he always said that our child would come into the role when we least expect them too . Now look this was happening like he had said and all . But I was thankful for this . But this pain was worser than having your period .

Giovanni gets to the hospital and waiting for her and little Isabella was her Doctor and all. They were ready to deliver this precious angel. Giovanni look down and say sweet princess we are about to bring you out to this world good on baby mama and daddy both love you so much . Isabella kick so that meant she understood what was going on . The doctor said we are ready for you both and I plan on taking care of you both .

Smiling through the mask she had on . Giovanni nodded through another contraction. They were coming closer and closer together . But they knew why . She hadn't even pack her baby bag but her baby Uncle Rod went to her home and pack a bag for her and got all of Isabella stuff .

Family has to stick together during this . This was the perfect time to be here for her and all . She couldn't helped but to smile . But in a moment would be the time to push . Giovanni was over there praying and being pray for by Mimi aka Mary David Sims mama . She said safe delivery and safe recovery too in Jesus name . Amen .

Giovanni like that she was spiritual. She knew she was in good hands like nationwide . Something that she always knew . The doctor said alright Giovanni push baby . Giovanni push like her life depend on it . They said we see the head and told her stop pushing and she was listening .

She didn't know if it was the meds or what but standing in the corner she look and saw David in all white suit and he said push baby . You got this . Giovanni kept pushing until she heard the baby crying .

Hearing that crying let her know little mama has made her appearance . Isabella Marie Sims was finally HERE . Giovanni crying tears of joy and pain and happiness and sadness too . She had did this by herself .

Giovanni held her baby girl and said hey little mama I'm you're mama . At that moment she felt all she needed too . To protect and love and care for her child . One who was created by love and would be protected by love too .

Isabella Marie Sims weight 9lbs and 12 oz and 22.5 inches long . She smiled big because she knew she was in a room filled with love and prayers . She was healthy but this little sassy girl was HUNGRY and let it be known . Giovanni said acting just like her daddy David . The first person to touch her was her Mimi after Giovanni feed her .

So much love was in that woman that made her happy that this was something that was beautiful . You're my little princess and know you will always be protected by this family and your mama family always . That's what your daddy would have want for you and your mama .

Giovanni cried but she knew Mimi had meant every single word and knew things would get better for them over time and this was one of those things that would helped them grow in love and not with hatred.

Thank you David ! Giovanni said in a whisper but then his mama said he is here isn't he ? She said yes he is and she said tell my son I love him and will protect Isabella forever. Giovanni said he knows and he is at peace now he said justice was served .

Giovanni was the Unapologetic Black Woman because she had defeated all odds and had her baby without the father and stood through it all . She didn't want to apologize about how she felt about how the police took her future and her mate away . She knew that since she felt this way she had to do what was best for her .

At that moment she decided to take over David's Business and renamed David Unapologetic Sims . Liking the new name called the business man who he had last dealt with he was excited to be working with Giovanni and along with the Black

Lives Movement . Things were going to be

alright with them after all .

Giovanni WON respect from the nation

and she won the respect of her family and

friends . She was happy but deep down

she was missing her baby David . She

hung a picture of him in Isabella room and

made her smile and happy .

The Unapologetic Black Woman was

Giovanni Shanice Reid and she dealt with

this death better than she thought . She is

now a mother and she had a princess who

is looking at her for guidance and how she handles herself .

Giovanni and Isabella were going to be alright and could handle anything together . Their bond would be the strongest one to the word . David would have been happy about what's happened . At the end of this story he wasn't just another hashtag he was MORE than that .

He was apart of the movement that many have been on but not all got the justice that they needed or even want at all . But at the end of the day David's life meant a lot to his family and friends and including his daughter . So remember and say his #DAVIDSIMS .

May your life continue to lived. We won't forget about you at all. The BLM will continue to speak your name and hold it on our heart . Our movement will be one of greatest .

This book is in dedication for the many

lives that have died while the Black Lives

Matters Movement :

#BreonnaTaylor

#GeorgeFloyd

#AhmaudArbery

#SandraBland

#FreddieGrey

#EricGarner

#MichaelBrown

#TamirRice

#PhilandoCastile

#BothamJean

#AtatianaJefferson

May we remember these names lives that were taken too soon . May they all get justice and the killing stops .